Tadpoles

Rooster's
Alarm

Crabtree Publishing Company
www.crabtreebooks.com
1-800-387-7650

PMB 16A, 350 Fifth Ave.
Suite 3308,
New York, NY

616 Welland Ave.
St. Catharines, ON
L2M 5V6

Published by Crabtree Publishing in 2010

Series Editor: Jackie Hamley
Editor: Reagan Miller
Series Advisor: Dr. Hilary Minns
Series Designer: Peter Scoulding
Editorial Director: Kathy Middleton

First published in 2008
by Franklin Watts
(A division of Hachette
Children's Books)

**Library and Archives Canada
Cataloguing in Publication**

Available at Library and Archives Canada

**Library of Congress
Cataloging-in-Publication Data**

Smith, Ian.
  Rooster's alarm / by Ian Smith and Sean Julian ;
illustrated by Ian Smith.
    p. cm. -- (Tadpoles)
  Summary: When a sheep cries "Cock-a-doodle-
doo" to awaken the other animals, each responds
with a surprising sound, while all wonder where
the rooster has gone.
  ISBN 978-0-7787-3905-0 (pbk.) -- ISBN
978-0-7787-3874-9 (reinforced library binding)
  [1. Stories in rhyme. 2. Animal sounds--Fiction.
3. Domestic animals--Fiction.] I. Julian, Sean.
II. Title. III. Series.

  PZ8.3.S6516Roo 2010
  [E]--dc22
                                    2009025302

Rooster's Alarm

by Ian Smith and Sean Julian

Illustrated by Ian Smith

Crabtree Publishing Com

www.crabtreebooks.com

Sean Julian

"I don't like
alarm clocks
because they
wake me up when
I still want to
be asleep."

Ian Smith

"I set my
alarm clock
good and early so
I can get up and
have a nice cup
of tea."

"Cock-a-doodle-doo!"
cried the sheep,

Cock-a-doodle-doo!

waking up the animals
who were still asleep.

6

The cat woke up and opened his eyes.

He began to baa
to his great surprise.

The mouse meowed,

Meow!

and the dog said, "Squeak!"

Squeak!

The turkey barked, "Woof!" when he opened his beak.

The goat yelled, "Moo!"

Moo!

14

But that is what the horse was going to say.

So the horse said,
"Oink!"

Oink!

And the pig began to cluck.

Quack! Quack!

That made the hen
quack, just like the
duck.

The noises were wrong
all around the farm,

22

because the rooster
forgot to set his alarm!

Notes for adults

TADPOLES are structured to provide support for early readers. The stories may also be used by adults for sharing with young children.

Starting to read alone can be daunting. **TADPOLES** help by providing visual support and repeating high frequency words and phrases. These books will both develop confidence and encourage reading and rereading for pleasure.

If you are reading this book with a child, here are a few suggestions:

1. Make reading fun! Choose a time to read when you and the child are relaxed and have time to share the story.
2. Talk about the story before you start reading. Look at the cover and the blurb. What might the story be about? Why might the child like it?
3. Encourage the child to reread the story, and to retell the story in their own words, using the illustrations to remind them what has happened.
4. Discuss the story and see if the child can relate it to their own experiences, or perhaps compare it to another story they know.
5. Give praise! Children learn best in a positive environment.

If you enjoyed this book, why not try another TADPOLES story?

At the End of the Garden
9780778738503 RLB
9780778738817 PB

Bad Luck, Lucy!
9780778738510 RLB
9780778738824 PB

Ben and the Big Balloon
9780778738602 RLB
9780778738916 PB

Crabby Gabby
9780778738527 RLB
9780778738831 PB

Dad's Cake
9780778738657 RLB
9780778738961 PB

Dad's Van
9780778738664 RLB
9780778738978 PB

The Dinosaur Next Door
9780778738732 RLB
9780778739043 PB

Five Teddy Bears
9780778738534 RLB
9780778738848 PB

I'm Taller Than You!
9780778738541 RLB
9780778738855 PB

Leo's New Pet
9780778738558 RLB
9780778738862 PB

Little Troll
9780778738565 RLB
9780778738879 PB

Mop Top
9780778738572 RLB
9780778738886 PB

My Auntie Susan
9780778738589 RLB
9780778738893 PB

My Big, New Bed
9780778738596 RLB
9780778738909 PB

Night, Night
9780778738671 RLB
9780778738985 PB

Over the Moon!
9780778738688 RLB
9780778738992 PB

Pirate Pete
9780778738619 RLB
9780778738923 PB

Rooster's Alarm
9780778738749 RLB
9780778739050 PB

Runny Honey
9780778738626 RLB
9780778738930 PB

The Sad Princess
9780778738725 RLB
9780778739036 PB

Sammy's Secret
9780778738633 RLB
9780778738947 PB

Sam's Sunflower
9780778738640 RLB
9780778738954 PB

Tag!
9780778738695 RLB
9780778739005 PB

Ted's Party Bus
9780778738701 RLB
9780778739012 PB

Tortoise Races Home
9780778738718 RLB
9780778739029 PB

Printed in the USA—CG